© 2010 Disney Enterprises, Inc.
Published by Hachette Partworks Ltd
ISBN: 978-1-906965-35-8
Date of Printing: February 2010
Printed in Singapore by Tien Wah Press

Disney PRINCESS

POCAHONTAS

Disney

H hachette

At the London docks a ship called the *Susan Constant* was about to sail for America – the New World!

The sailors said goodbye to their wives.

But John Smith did not say goodbye to anyone.

He lived only for adventure.

Their leader, Governor Ratcliffe, arrived with his pampered dog named Percy. The greedy Ratcliffe was going to America to find gold!

Soon they were all sailing across the sea.

John Smith became friends
with Thomas, a young man who
wanted to settle in America. Thomas
had never been to sea before.

Thomas learned that crossing the
ocean was very dangerous. During a
terrible storm he was swept overboard!

"Help!" cried Thomas. "Save me!"

John Smith quickly jumped into the crashing waves to save his friend.

Soon they were both safely back on board the ship.

"That was refreshing," Smith joked. The brave men sailed on to the New World.

But America was not a new world to the peaceful
people already living there.

One tribe was led by Chief Powhatan. He had a
beautiful daughter named Pocahontas.

Pocahontas loved to have fun. She also loved
exploring the river with her animal friends.
 Meeko, a raccoon, was even more mischievous
than his human friend. A hummingbird named
Flit tried to keep them both out of trouble.

One day Pocahontas went to the Enchanted Glade to talk to Grandmother Willow. The magical tree was very wise.

Pocahontas told Grandmother Willow her problem.

"My father wants me to marry Kocoum. But Kocoum is such a serious warrior. What should I do?"

"You must follow your own path," Grandmother Willow advised.

"But how will I find my path?" Pocahontas asked.

The wise tree answered, "You must listen with your heart."

So Pocahontas listened. She listened very hard.

Then she heard two words: *strange clouds*.

Pocahontas climbed to the top of Grandmother Willow. There *were* strange clouds!

The "clouds" were the white sails of a big ship.
Pocahontas ran to the river. She saw four pale
men in a smaller boat. The men were rowing
towards the shore.

Pocahontas had never seen men like these
before. And the sailors had never seen such a
beautiful place. John Smith couldn't wait to
explore this amazing new land.

Smith jumped out of the
boat. Thomas and two settlers named Ben
and Lon tied the boat to a rock.

Smith climbed a nearby tree.

Pocahontas watched him. She had never seen yellow hair before.

Pocahontas thought the stranger looked friendly, but she wasn't sure. So she stayed hidden.

But Meeko thought the stranger might have
food. He walked right up to John Smith!

Smith had never seen a raccoon before.
"You're a strange-looking fellow," he told
Meeko.

Smith reached into his bag. "Would you like
a biscuit?"

Meeko liked the biscuit very much!

Back in the village, the rest of the tribe had already learned about the strangers' arrival.

Kekata, the medicine man, said the strange men were beasts, different from the Powhatan people.

Chief Powhatan sent some warriors to watch the newcomers. He told the rest of his people to stay away from them. "Let us hope the strangers do not intend to stay," he added.

Powhatan didn't know that Pocahontas and
Meeko were still following John Smith! Pocahontas
was curious. And Meeko wanted more biscuits.

John Smith had never seen such a wonderful
land. America was wild and free! He stopped
at a beautiful waterfall. Suddenly Smith heard
something close by. He looked around.

Pocahontas hid behind the waterfall.

Smith could see a figure beyond the water. He aimed his gun, ready to shoot!

Pocahontas couldn't see Smith any longer. She stepped out into the open.

Smith was surprised. He had expected to see a
fierce warrior. Instead, he saw a lovely girl!
    Pocahontas and John Smith stared into each
other's eyes.

Meanwhile, Kocoum and the other warriors were
watching the strangers.

The settlers had started building a fort. And
they were already digging for gold. The men cut
down trees and tore up the earth.

"Dig faster!" greedy Governor Ratcliffe ordered.
When the settlers noticed the warriors, they shot
at them! One of the braves was injured.

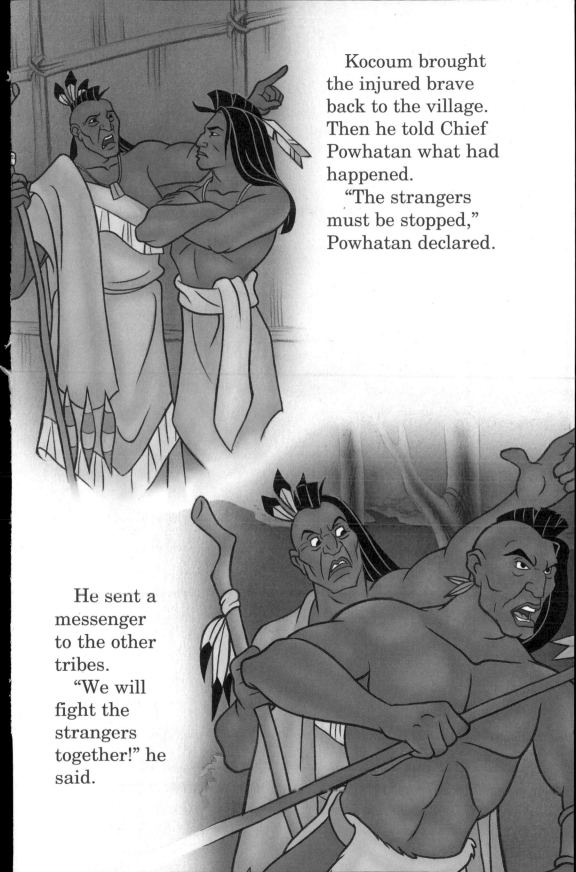

Kocoum brought the injured brave back to the village. Then he told Chief Powhatan what had happened.

"The strangers must be stopped," Powhatan declared.

He sent a messenger to the other tribes.

"We will fight the strangers together!" he said.

Pocahontas and John Smith were no longer
strangers. Smith showed Pocahontas how to shake
hands.

Pocahontas remembered Grandmother Willow's
words: *Listen with your heart*.

So Pocahontas listened.

Their hands touched.

Suddenly Pocahontas could understand John
Smith's words! And he could understand hers.

Smith told Pocahontas about London. "It has streets filled with carriages and buildings as tall as trees."

Pocahontas said, "I would like to see those things."

Smith smiled. "You will. We're going to build them here." He thought Pocahontas would be pleased, but she was angry!

Pocahontas liked the way she lived. "The earth is not a dead thing you can own. We are all part of nature," she told him.

As Pocahontas spoke, Smith began to see the world through her eyes. And it was the most fascinating world he had ever seen!

Smith returned to the fort. But he wanted to see Pocahontas again. So the next day he found Pocahontas in a cornfield outside her village.

Pocahontas brought him to the Enchanted Glade.

"What a beautiful place," John sighed. "To think we came all this way just to dig it up for gold."

Pocahontas asked, "What is gold?"

Smith showed her some gold coins. Pocahontas shook her head. "There is nothing like that here." She showed Smith an ear of corn. "This is the only gold here. But it tastes good." Smith had to agree.

Then Smith heard a voice say, "Hello, John Smith. Come closer." He looked up. The tree was talking to him!

Pocahontas introduced him to Grandmother Willow.

"He has a good soul. And he's handsome, too!" the wise tree told Pocahontas.

Smith grinned. "I like her!" he said.

Suddenly Smith heard Ben and Lon calling him.
He was afraid his friends might hurt Pocahontas.

"We can't let them see us," he whispered to
Pocahontas. They hid behind the big tree.

As the men approached, Grandmother Willow
used her roots to trip Ben and Lon!

"That tree moved!" Ben shouted. They were so
scared, they ran away.

Pocahontas and Smith agreed to meet that night. Then they both hurried home.

When Pocahontas reached her village, she saw warriors from many other tribes. They were all ready for war!

Pocahontas said, "Father, we do not have to fight. There must be a better path."

But Chief Powhatan saw no other way to save the land.

John Smith tried to stop the war, too.

Governor Ratcliffe would not listen. "The Indians have our gold. And I'm going to get it!"

"But there is no gold!" Smith cried.

Ratcliffe did not believe him. He decided to attack the tribes and seize their gold.

That night,
Smith met
Pocahontas.
They knew
that somehow
they had to
stop the war.
They kissed.

Suddenly Kocoum came rushing out of
the woods. He thought the stranger would
hurt Pocahontas.

Pocahontas cried, "Kocoum, no!"
Then someone else came out of the woods.
Thomas had followed Smith. He was afraid
Kocoum would hurt Smith. Thomas raised his gun
and fired!
"Thomas, don't!" Smith shouted.
But it was too late. Kocoum was dead.

Other warriors heard the shot.
"Run, Thomas! Run!" Smith shouted.
Thomas escaped. But the angry warriors
captured Smith. They dragged him to the village.

Kocoum's
body was
brought back
to the village.
Everyone in
the tribe was
very angry!

Chief Powhatan said, "At sunrise, this stranger will die."

Pocahontas went to John Smith. "I am so sorry. This would never have happened if we had not met," she said.

"I would rather die tomorrow than live a hundred years without knowing you," Smith said softly.

Pocahontas knew she had to save him. But how?

At dawn the warriors took Smith to a tall cliff.
Ratcliffe and the settlers were there, too. Both
sides were ready for war!

Chief Powhatan raised his war club.

Then Pocahontas ran up. She threw herself between her father and John Smith.

"If you kill him, you will have to kill me, too. I love him, Father!" Pocahontas cried.

Chief Powhatan was surprised.

"Look around you," Pocahontas said. "This is where the path of hatred leads."

Chief Powhatan put down his club.
"My daughter speaks with wisdom. She comes
here with courage and understanding," he said.
Powhatan told his braves to let Smith go.
The braves and settlers lowered their weapons.

But Ratcliffe wanted his gold and his war.

"Now is our chance! Shoot!" he ordered. But the settlers wouldn't shoot. So Ratcliffe grabbed a gun and fired at Chief Powhatan.

John Smith saw what was happening.

He jumped between the bullet and the chief!

The bullet hit Smith in the stomach. Pocahontas cradled the wounded man in her arms.

"You shot him!" Thomas shouted at Ratcliffe.

"It's his own fault," Ratcliffe spluttered. But the settlers knew Ratcliffe was wrong.

The settlers tied up Ratcliffe and sent him back to England.

Smith was carried back to the ship. He felt no pain. All he felt was love for Pocahontas and her wild, free land.

Smith looked into Pocahontas's eyes. "Come with me?" he asked.

Pocahontas wanted to go with Smith. But she had to stay. She had found her path. Pocahontas would keep peace between the settlers and her tribe.

Smith wanted to stay. But he had to go back. The doctors in England could heal his wound.

Pocahontas wished she and Smith could stay together. But she knew it did not matter where they lived. They would always be together in their hearts.